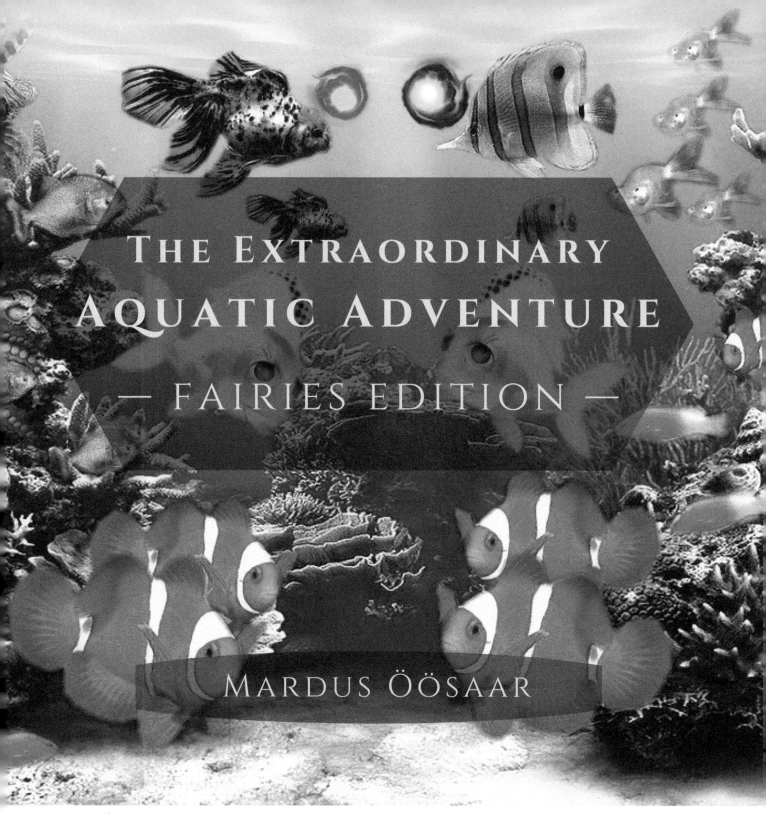

The Extraordinary Aquatic Adventure

— Fairies Edition —

Mardus Öösaar

IT WAS A WONDERFULLY WARM DAY. BENJAMIN THE
FAIRY FLOATED THROUGH THE FOREST,
ALL CREATURES, BIG AND SMALL WERE FROLLICKING
AROUND.

THAT DAY, HOWEVER, SOMETHING
EXTRAORDINARY WAS FOUND

THE BEAR AND BENJAMIN NOTICED SOMETHING BLUE
GLOWING ON THE GROUND.

ODDLY ENOUGH, IT WAS A LIGHT BULB FILLED WITH
WATER AND TINY CREATURES

TO INVESTIGATE, BENJAMIN INVITED HIS FRIEND IRIS
AND BEFORE THEY COULD COUNT TO TEN, THEIR MAGIC
POWERS TRANSPORTED THEM INTO THE FASCINATING
AQUATIC WORLD

ALL OF A SUDDEN, THEY WERE SURROUNDED BY WATER.
THEY ENCOUNTERED A FUNNY SWARM OF FISH

HE SAID THAT EVERYONE IN THE LIGHTBULB LAND WAS
HAVING PROBLEMS AND ASKED IF THE JOLLY FAIRIES
COULD ACCOMPANY HIM TO THE KING OF THIS
KINGDOM. THE FAIRIES WERE MORE THAN HAPPY TO GO.

THE FISH AND HIS FRIENDS TOOK OUR FAIRIES TO THE KING'S CHAMBERS AND SWAM OFF TO GET SOME FOOD.

THE KING OF THIS LAND WAS AN OLD WISE TOAD..
HE WAS VERY CONCERNED WITH THE WELL BEING OF
THE SEA FOLK LIVING IN THE BULB.

HE KINDLY ASKED IF THE FAIRIES COULD GO AROUND
AND TALK WITH THE SEA CREATURES AND HELP THEM
SOLVE THEIR PROBLEMS

After the formal meeting with the king, the
Chancellor of the Light Bulb nation came to.
meet the two fairies.
Iris was getting all excited to meet all of these
important creatures.

The Great Turtle took the friends on a tour of
the Kingdom.

FIRST, THE CHANCELLOR TOOK THE FAIRIES TO SEE HIS COUSIN REDDY. HE WAS FEELING DOWN BECAUSE HIS SHELL WAS A BIT TOO TIGHT.

THE FRIENDLIEST DOLPHIN FOUND THE FAIRIES'
TOUR AND CAME TO SAY HOW SHE WISHED SHE
COULD FLY FREE IN THE SKY OUTSIDE
OF THE BULB KINGDOM.

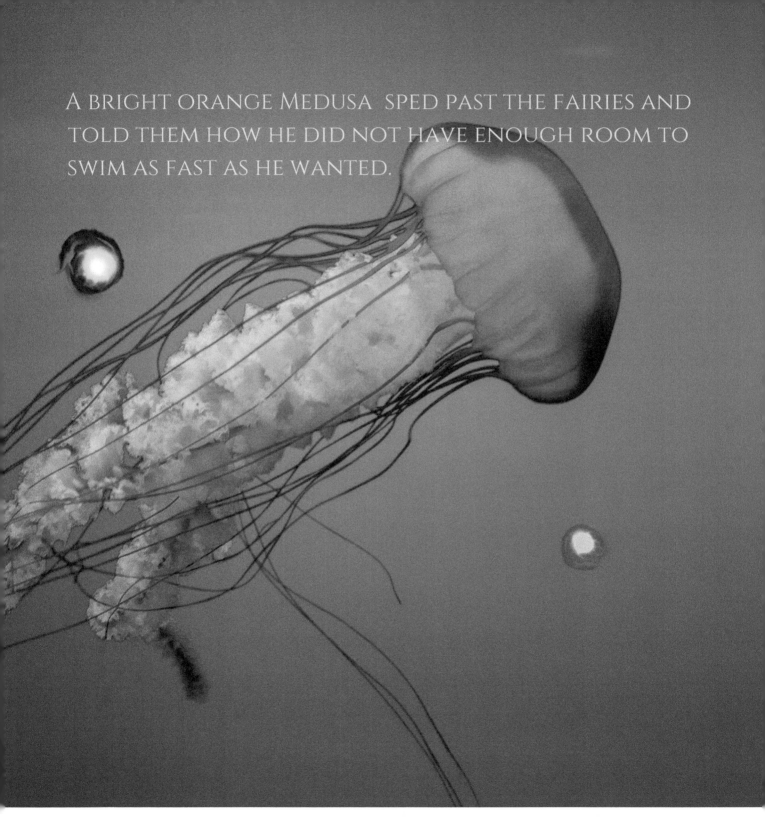

A BRIGHT ORANGE MEDUSA SPED PAST THE FAIRIES AND
TOLD THEM HOW HE DID NOT HAVE ENOUGH ROOM TO
SWIM AS FAST AS HE WANTED.

THEY DRIFTED DEEPER AND DEEPER
INTO THE DEEP ABYSS.
AS THEY NEARED THE BOTTOM, A FLAT-NOSED SHARK
TOLD THEM IT WAS TOO DARK TO SEE CLEARLY.

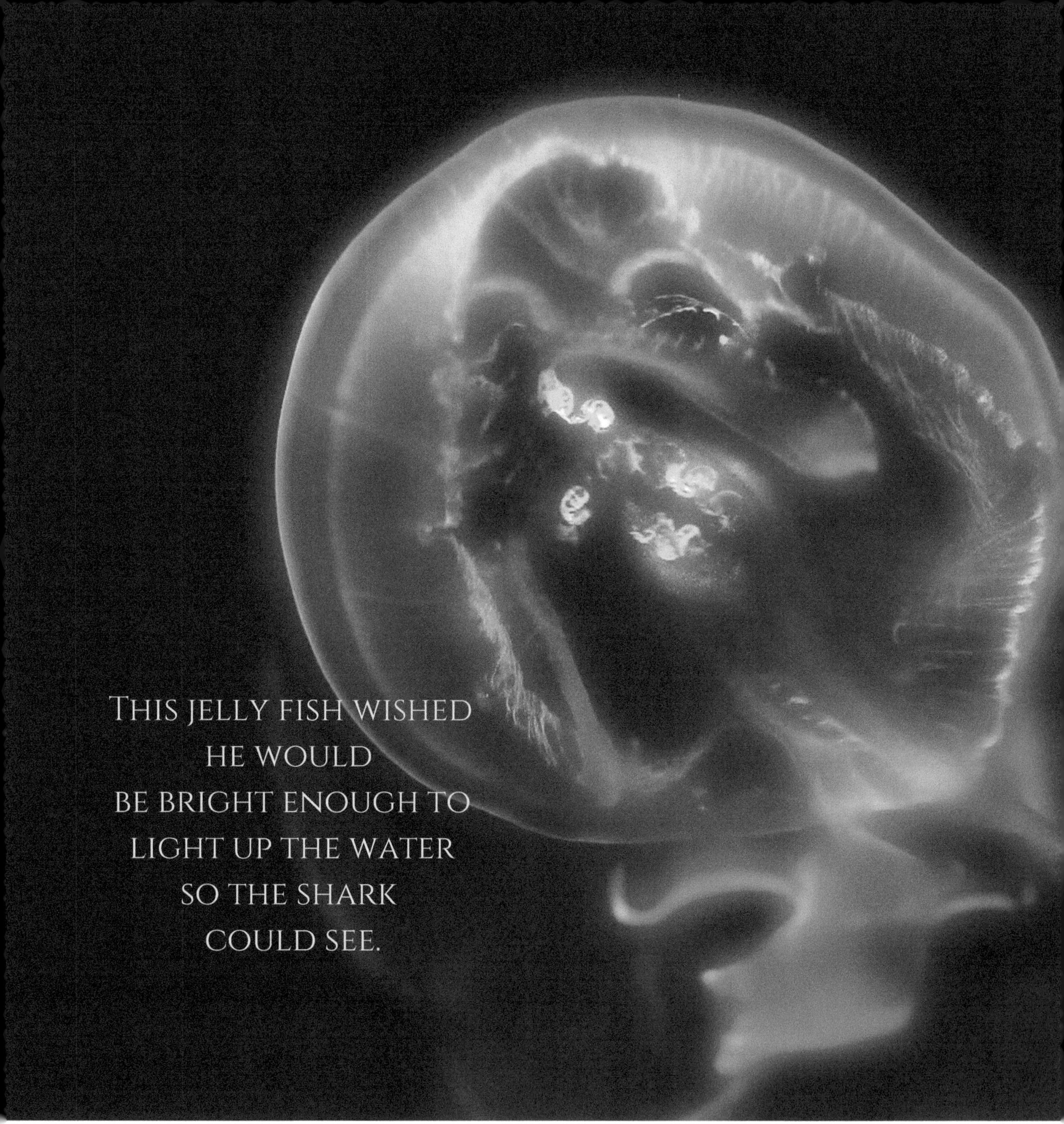

THIS JELLY FISH WISHED
HE WOULD
BE BRIGHT ENOUGH TO
LIGHT UP THE WATER
SO THE SHARK
COULD SEE.

THE WATER WAS QUITE DEEP NOW
AND IT BECAME A LITTLE
HARDER TO BREATHE,

SO THE CHANCELLOR MR. TURTLE
HEAD BACK TO FULFILL HIS DUTIES.

UNSURPRISINGLY, THIS PART OF THE
KINGDOM WAS EVER SO
FASCINATING..

THE CORAL REEF WAS TEEMING WITH LIFE. HOWEVER,
THE PINK CORALS WISHED THEY COULD SWING IN
THE SWEET WIND OUTSIDE.

A CURIOUS LITTLE YELLOW FISH CAME TO GREET THE
FAIRIES AND OFFERED QUITE AN INTRIGUING IDEA.

HE SAID THERE WAS A MERMAID WHO LIVED DEEP IN THE
CORAL REEF. SHE HAD THE POWER TO HELP EVERYONE.

Benjamin and Iris searched far and wide, scavaging the deepest parts of this magical place. They encountered a whole variety of unbelievable sights.

An Underwater Cellist Finally found someone who would listen to his melodies.

AFTER A LONG DAY OF SEARCHING THEY FOUND POSEIDON THE GOD OF SEAS. HE STOOD TALL WITH HIS TRIDENT AND WAS AS FRIENDLY AS A LAMB.

He told them that his trident wielded the power to grant any wish of the fairies.

This was a gift to the fairies for being so kind to everyone for such a long time.

The unsuspecting fairies wished that the wishes of all the merfolk they had met be fulfilled.

ON THAT VERY INSTANT A BRIGHT WHITE
LIGHT SHONE DOWN UPON THE SEA
CREATURES.

EVERYONE WAS FREED FROM THE MAGICAL LIGHT BULB
AND SET FREE TO ROAM THE EARTH.

NOW THE FLAT-NOSED SHARK HAD ALL THE LIGHT IN THE WORLD. HE COULD SEE EXACTLY WHERE HE WAS GOING.

REDDY THE TURTLE HAD A WONDERFUL GARDEN
GROWING ON HIS SHELL TO HELP HIM RELAX

SOME OF THESE MAGICAL CREATURES STILL ROAM THE
PLANET AND HAVE BECOME LEGENDARY.

WHILE TRAVELLING BACK
TO FAIRYLAND, T
HE TWO FRIENDS DISCUSSED:

IT'S IMPORTANT TO BE MINDFUL
OF WHAT YOU WISH FOR.

**BECAUSE YOU JUST MIGHT
GET IT!**

Fairies In The Desert

The Quest For The Law of Supply

Written by Mardus Öösaar

Benjamin the fairy descended from some snowy
mountains to meet his friend Iris.
They were so surprised to find a very dry and
arid desert.

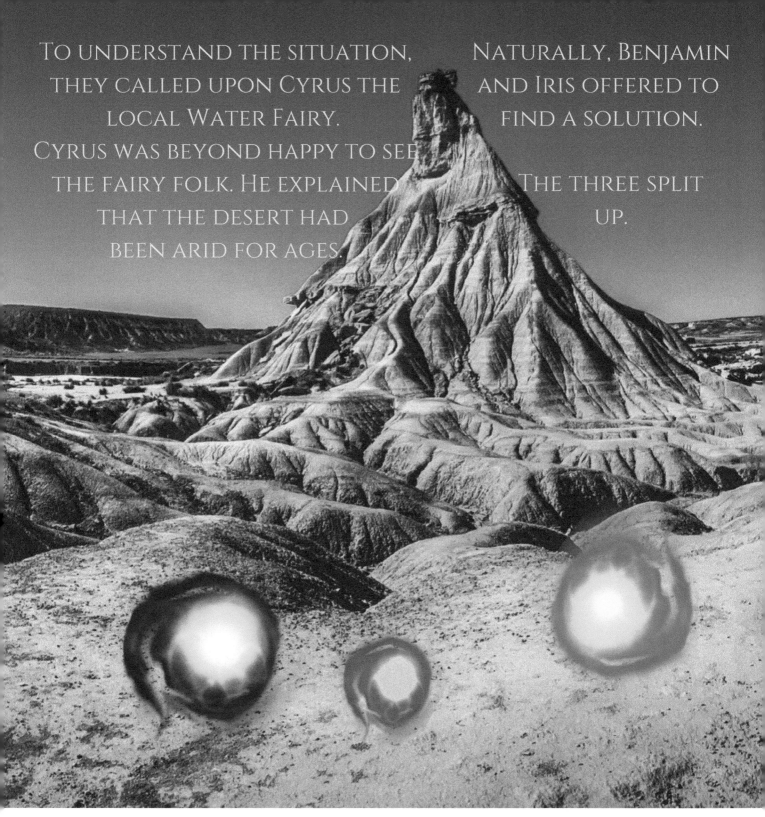

To understand the situation, they called upon Cyrus the local Water Fairy. Cyrus was beyond happy to see the fairy folk. He explained that the desert had been arid for ages.

Naturally, Benjamin and Iris offered to find a solution.

The three split up.

BENJAMIN FLEW EAST TO SEE WHICH ANIMALS HE COULD
POSSIBLY ASK FOR INFORMATION.

HE ENCOUNTERED A RESTING
MEERKAT.
THE MEERKAT SAID HE HAD NOT
SEEN A DROP OF RAIN IN YEARS
AND THAT HE WISHED HE COULD
SPLASH AROUND IN THE
PUDDLES AS ONCE LONG AGO

A friendly Desert Goat wandered by the Meerkat and Benjamin and added to the story. There used to be a river flowing through these parts and now it has been lost for many years.

Benjamin let out an Echo to send this new information to Iris and Cyrus using his fairy powers.

AS SOON AS IRIS HEARD OF THIS, SHE ASKED THE
SHARP-EYED HAWK TO FLY AROUND THE DESERT TO
TRY AND SPOT ANY REMNANTS OF A RIVER.

ALTHOUGH THE WISE OLD IGUANA DID NOT MIND IT BEING DRY.

CYRUS, ON THE OTHER HAND, CAME ACROSS A PACK ON JOURNEYING ELEPHANTS. THEY WERE WELL ON THEIR WAY TO FINDING A WATER SUPPLY.

THE PACK OF ELEPHANTS HAD BEEN ON THEIR WAY FOR MONTHS. BY THEIR CHEERFUL PACE IT SEEMED THAT THEY HAD ALMOST ARRIVED. THIS WAS A SURE SIGN THAT THERE WOULD BE WATER NEARBY!

MR. MONGOOSE WISHED TO MOISTEN UP HIS FUR COAT,
BUT UNFORTUNATELY THERE WASN'T A SINGLE DROP OF
RAIN THIS SEASON!

ON THE OTHER HAND, THE DESERT LYNX NEVER LOST HOPE THAT ONE DAY THEY WOULD FIND A WHOLE LOAD OF FLOWING WATER.

THIS THIRSTY LION WAS AT A LOSS FOR WORDS .
BENJAMIN MADE A PROMISE TO FIND SOME
WATER FOR EVERYONE.

THE LION CUB HAD YET TO SEE A BODY OF WATER.
THE NATURE WAS SPARCE AND NO RAIN HAD OCCURRED
AS LONG AS HE COULD REMEMBER.

DESPITE THERE BEING NO WATER THE GIRAFFE SPECIES COULD STILL GRASP THE HIGH TREES AS A VALUABLE FOOD SUPPLY.

THEY EXCEL AT REACHING HIGH PLACES!

UNTIL SHE COMES OF AGE, THE GIRAFFE BABY WILL REPRESENT THE LOOKOUT SQUAD!

OUR HIGH-PATROL BIRD RETURNED WITH SOME GREAT NEWS. HE COULD INDICATE THE DIRECTION OF OUR SOON-TO-BE WATER SUPPLY!

THIS CREATED EXCITEMENT AMONG THE DESERT DWELLERS AS MORE ANIMALS JOINED THE SEARCH.

THE RESTED
MEERKAT PROVIDED
WONDERFUL
INSIGHT FROM A
LOWER PERSPECTIVE.

HE FOUND LOFTY
VEGETATION AND
GREEN PLANTS!

THE PERSISTENT DESERT ANIMALS AND HELPFUL
FAIRIES UNCOVERED A SACRED RIVER THAT WAS
FLOWING IN ITS OWN COURSE FOR CENTURIES
WITHOUT DISCOVERY.

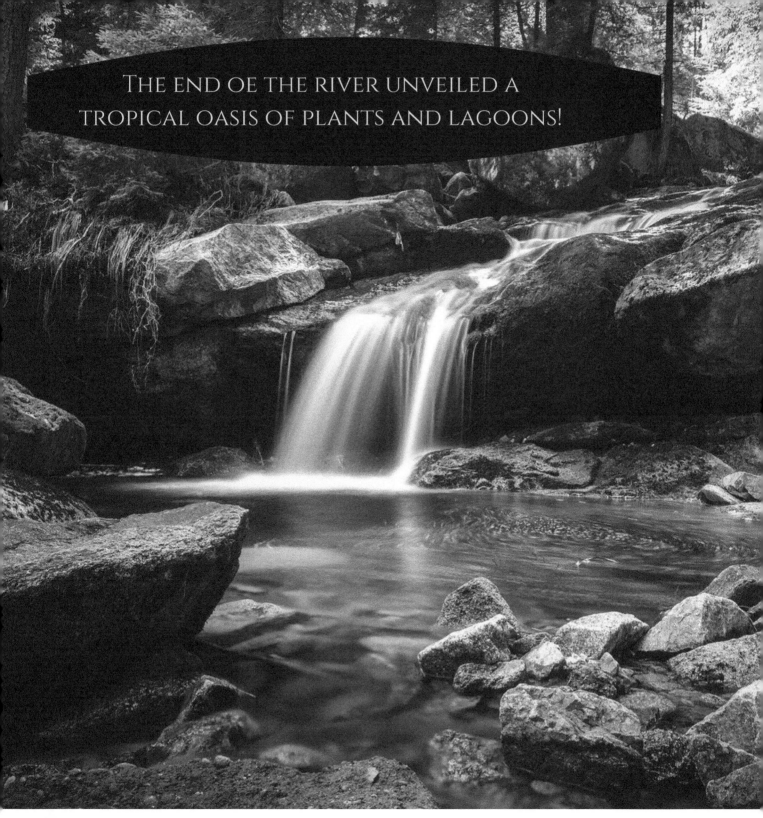

THE END OE THE RIVER UNVEILED A
TROPICAL OASIS OF PLANTS AND LAGOONS!

MOST LIKELY THE ANIMALS HAD
BEEN LIVING IN THEIR COMFORT
ZONES ALL THIS TIME.
IT DID NOT TAKE MUCH TIME UNTIL
ALL THE ANIMALS DECIDED TO TAKE
THE EXTRA STEP INTO THE
UNKNOWN.

IT WAS A TRUE JOY FOR THE MIGHTY LION TO COOL DOWN HIS PAWS IN THE MOIST SPRINGY MUD!

AS EXPECTED, THE COURAGEOUS DESERT LYNX LEAD THE PURSUIT AND SUPPORTED THE DESERT DWELLERS WITH CONFIDENCE.

THE ELEPHANTS HAD ENOUGH WATER TO RELAX AND BATHE WITH THE WHOLE FAMILY!

THE ANIMALS STAYED FOR A WHILE TO REST, PLAY AND EART. BUT AS THEY GREW CONTENT, THEY DECIDED TO HEAD BACK TO THE DESERT. THEY NOW KNEW HOW TO COME BACK ANYTIME!

THE FAIRIES KNEW VERY WELL THEY HAD SUCCEEDED IN TEACHING THE WORLD TRUE KNOWLEDGE OF THE LAW OF SUPPLY. TO PUT IT SIMPLY, TERE IS MORE THAN ENOUGH TO GO AROUND FOR EVERYBODY. EVEN IF IT DOES NOT SEEM LIKE IT AT FIRST. THIS IS AS TRUE AS THAT DAY ALWAYS FOLLOWS THE NIGHT!

BEAR IN MIND THAT
WHAT YOU CAN IMAGINE
AND WHAT YOU CAN
THINK, CAN ULTIMATELY
BECOME A REALITY.

THERE IS NO SHORTAGE
OF SUPPLY OUT THERE.
NOT MONETARY OR
OTHERWISE.

THERE IS ABUNDANCE
JUST WAITING FOR YOU
TO GO AND CLAIM IT.

YOU JUST HAVE TO BE
BOLD ENOUGH TO
DESIRE IT.

Original title:
Legacy of The Dragon:
Understanding
The Law of Forgiveness

Editor: Kristo Villem
Dedicated to Alfred Villem
ISBN 978-9949-7446-4-0

Legacy Of The Dragon

Understanding
The Law of Forgiveness

As long as history remembered, Dragons,
the might kings of the sky
had roamed the world of Fairyland.
It was said that most of them could fly with no
effort while others would never be blessed with
the gift of flight.

However, it is believed
that when one truly
desires something,
They cannot be denied of it.
After all, there is nothing
a fairy cannot grant, right?

This is Sparks. When he was born, nothing less than great was expected of him. He was witty, a wonderfully kind young dragon.
All of Fairyland adored him.

THE MORE HE GREW, THE MORE HE WOULD WAIT FOR HIS WINGS TO START GROWING.

ALL OF HIS FRIENDS WERE ALREADY FLOATING AROUND ABOVE THE GROUND.

Meanwhile, Benjamin the happy-go-lucky Fairy prepared for an afternoon stroll. He had heard that the Butterflies at Whimsical Woods had heard of something intriguing.
So he left his treehouse and floated on over.

THE WEATHER WAS SO FINE THAT HE
DECIDED TO TAKE THE LONG ROAD.

THIS MEANT HE PROBABLY WOULD NOT
MAKE IT BEFORE SUNDOWN.

He made it to The Whimsical Woods just as the
Moon shone brightest in the sky.

Now, you may think this is unfortunate, but it is
quite the contrary. The Butterflies living here
come out only during the night time.

BENJAMIN WAS TRULY CURIOUS TO HEAR THE TALES OF
THE MAGICAL BUTTERFLIES.
THE BIGGEST NEWS AROUND THESE PARTS WAS A YOUNG
NEWBORN DRAGON WHO HAD TROUBLE GROWING ITS
WINGS. GREEN DRAGONS ARE RARE IN THE WORLD AND
IT IS IMPORTANT THAT THEY CAN PATROL THE SKIES
FREELY. THIS GAVE BENJAMIN AN IDEA.

BENJAMIN LOOKED FAR AND WIDE FOR THIS INTRIGUING DRAGON.

DESPITE THERE BEING MANY STORIES OF HIS EXTRAORDINARY NATURAL SHINE, HE WAS NOT EASILIY FOUND.

Benjamin found Sparks on a branch . He was thinking deeply about life and was not in much of a mood for talking.

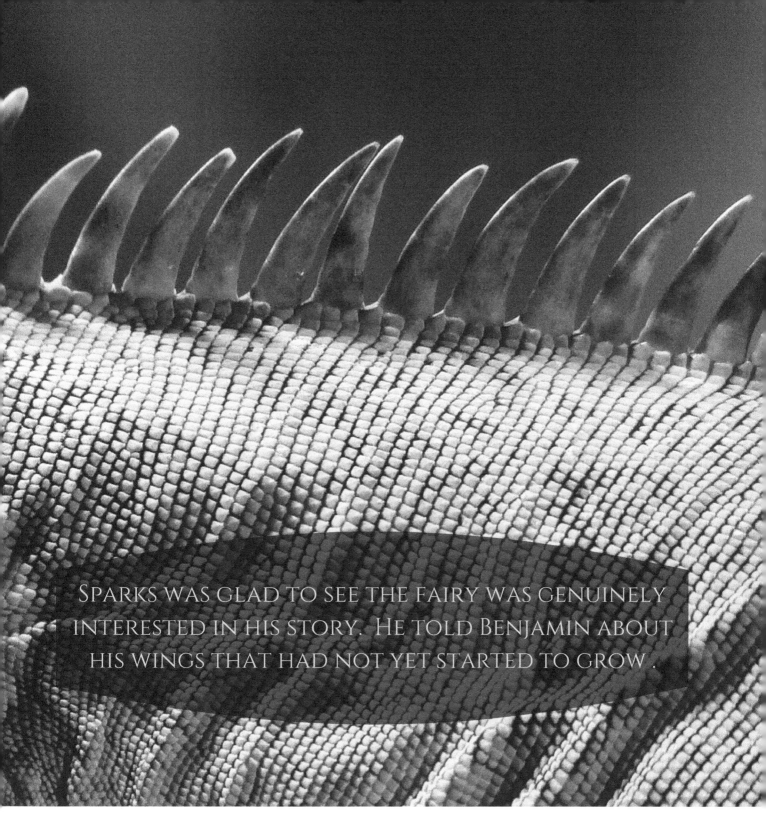

SPARKS WAS GLAD TO SEE THE FAIRY WAS GENUINELY
INTERESTED IN HIS STORY. HE TOLD BENJAMIN ABOUT
HIS WINGS THAT HAD NOT YET STARTED TO GROW.

BENJAMIN ASSURED HIM THAT NOTHING WAS IMPOSSIBLE AND THAT SPARKS SHOULD NOT FEEL DOWN ABOUT THIS. IN FACT, HE HAD A FRIEND WHO MIGHT BE ABLE TO HELP THE YOUNG DRAGON.

His old friend Reddy had been living in an ancient cave,
sharing his wisdom with only those who knew
where to find the huge old turtle.

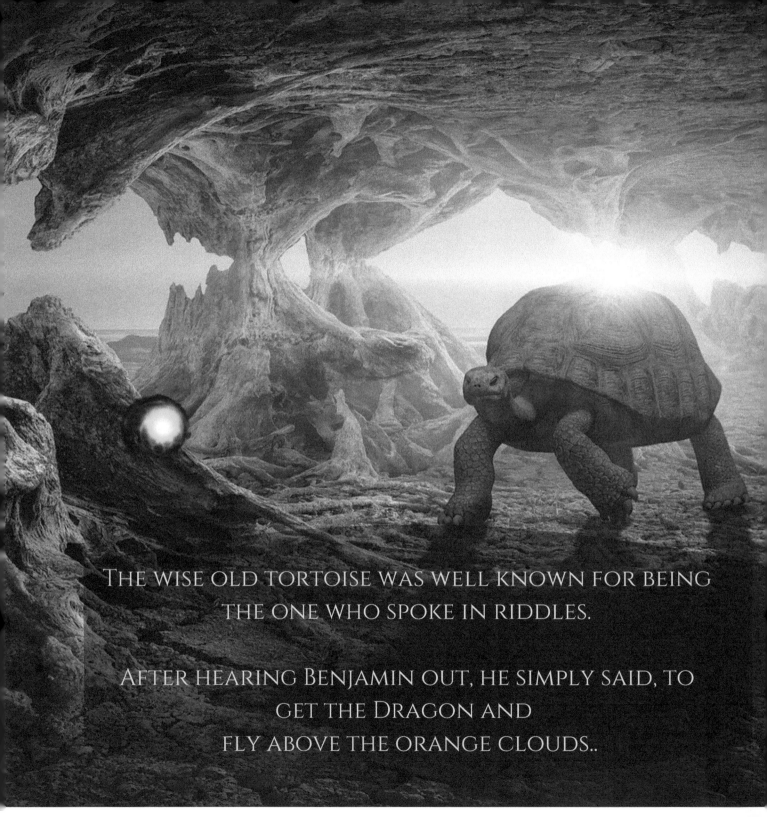

THE WISE OLD TORTOISE WAS WELL KNOWN FOR BEING
THE ONE WHO SPOKE IN RIDDLES.

AFTER HEARING BENJAMIN OUT, HE SIMPLY SAID, TO
GET THE DRAGON AND
FLY ABOVE THE ORANGE CLOUDS..

THEY DID AS BENJAMIN WAS TOLD AND SOON ENOUGH,
A WHOLE ARRAY OF TOWERS CAUGHT THE EYE.

After flying to a number of these towers, they had a particularily good feeling about one with a silver ornament.

THE DOOR WAS ONE OF GREAT STRENGTH.
IT OPENED AT ONCE WHEN THE TWO TRAVELLERS
CAME NEAR.

THE DOOR UNVEILED THE INSIDES OF A HUGE CASTLE. IN THIS CASTLE THERE WAS A MAGICAL TREE. THIS TREE GREW ORANGES THAT GLOWED BRIGHTLY THROUGH THE DARKNESS.

Benjamin had no doubt this was what Reddy was talking about. A single piece of fruit was enough to make the dragon's wings start growing rapidly.

NOT ONLY DID SPARKS' WINGS GROW BUT
HE GAINED IN SIZE REMARKABLY.

HE FLEW STRAIGHT OUT OF THE CASTLE TO FEEL THE
BREEZE IN THE WINGS FOR THE VERY FIRST TIME.

HE FLEW AROUND IN THE SUNLIT SKY FOR HOURS.
THIS FEELING OF FREEDOM WAS PRICELESS.

HOWEVER, THE MORE HE FLEW, THE SLOWER HE
THOUGHT HE BECAME. HE WAS SURE THIS WAS BECAUSE
THE MAGIC POWER OF THE ORANGE WAS RUNNING OUT.

BENJAMIN WAS JUST ON HIS WAY BACK TO HIS HOME AT
OAKVILLE WHEN HE SAW SPARKS THE DRAGON SOARING
EVER SO LOW JUST ABOVE THE TREES.

Sparks told Benjamin the magic of the Orange couldn't possibly carry him his whole life. That he should just give up on being a flying dragon.

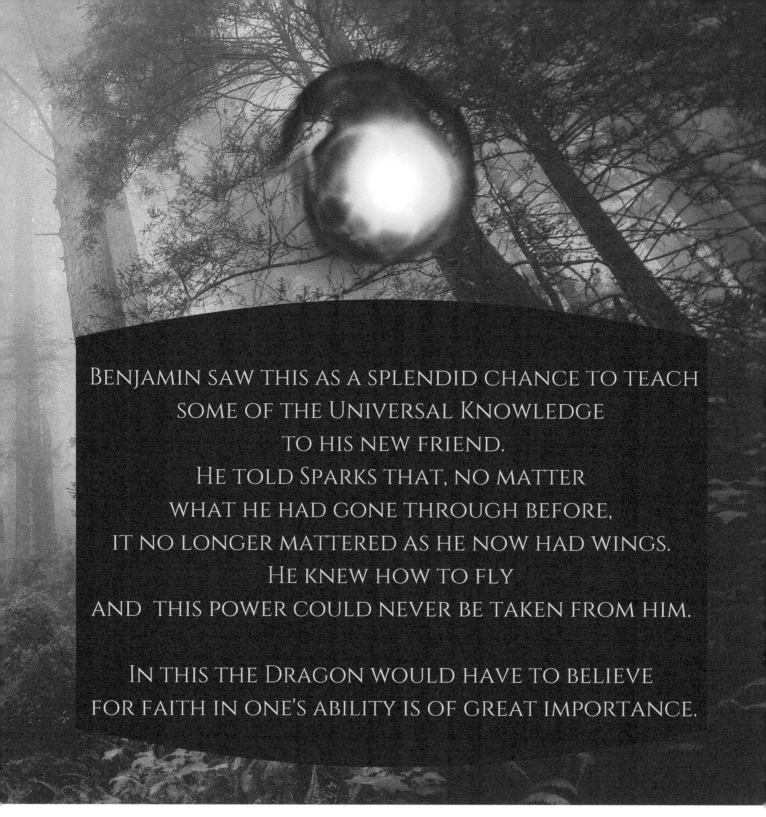

BENJAMIN SAW THIS AS A SPLENDID CHANCE TO TEACH
SOME OF THE UNIVERSAL KNOWLEDGE
TO HIS NEW FRIEND.
HE TOLD SPARKS THAT, NO MATTER
WHAT HE HAD GONE THROUGH BEFORE,
IT NO LONGER MATTERED AS HE NOW HAD WINGS.
HE KNEW HOW TO FLY
AND THIS POWER COULD NEVER BE TAKEN FROM HIM.

IN THIS THE DRAGON WOULD HAVE TO BELIEVE
FOR FAITH IN ONE'S ABILITY IS OF GREAT IMPORTANCE.

Sparks the Dragon would hear out
Benjamin's sound advice. He believed that he could
fly far and wide and so his self-trust
never again wavered.

Now, for centuries, Dragons roamed Fairyland
with great understanding that what they truly
learn would never fade.

TRUTH IS, EVERY ONE OF US
GOES THROUGH EXPERIENCES
THAT CAN BE, AT TIMES, HARD.

THIS WE CANNOT CHANGE.
HOWEVER, WE CAN CHANGE
OUR ATTITUDE TOWARDS HOW
THESE EXPERIENCES AFFECT US.

YOU SEE, WHAT BENJAMIN
TAUGHT SPARKS THE DRAGON
WAS THAT IN EVERY LAST
SITUATION IN LIFE, WE ALWAYS
DO OUR BEST, TO THE BEST OF
OUR KNOWLEDGE AND ABILITY.
EVEN IF SOMETHING GOES
WRONG, WE CAN ALWAYS
FORGIVE OURSELVES.

THAT IS THE UNIVERSAL
LAW OF FORGIVENESS.

CAM
Creative Arts Management

Thank You for reading This Book**!**

To show our **appreciation**, here is a **FREE** additional story about **Benjamin the Fairy!**

Download at:
www.creativeartsmanagement.org/
getyourbook/

MORE BOOKS by author Mardus Öösaar:

The Scandinavian Empires:
Nordic Wonders

Legacy Of The Dragon:
Understanding The Law of Forgiveness

Fairy of The Lost Continent:
The Sacred Law of Giving

Order at:

www.creativeartsmanagement.org

Lightning Source UK Ltd.
Milton Keynes UK
UKHW020741031220
374507UK00002B/95

9 789916 956632